Lick of the Lizard

Geraldine Mills

ARLEN HOUSE

Lick of the Lizard © Geraldine Mills, 2005

The moral right of the author has been asserted.

First published by Arlen House in September 2005

Arlen House
PO Box 222
Galway
Ireland
Phone/fax 086 8207617
arlenhouse@ireland.com

ISBN 1-903631-73-4, paperback
ISBN 1-903631-93-9, signed and numbered limited edition

Front cover: 'Energos 26' by Joan Hogan, courtesy of the artist
Back cover: 'Energos 22' by Joan Hogan, courtesy of the artist
Lizard photograph by Peter Moore
Typesetting: Arlen House
Printed by ColourBooks, Baldoyle, Dublin 13

Contents

Lick of the Lizard
7

Make My Bed, Light the Light
13

Walking Toby
21

Word-Eater
26

Gift of Mouth
32

Meal of Small Buttons
39

Osmosis
46

Dry Bones Time
52

World of Trees
59

Acknowledgements

'Lick of the Lizard' was winner of the OK award, 1999; the South Tipperary Short Story Award, 1999; shortlisted for the Francis MacManus Award in 1999; published in the *Sunday Tribune* 2000; winner of the Millennium *Sunday Tribune* Hennessy Emerging Fiction Award and overall winner of the New Irish Writer Award.

'Walking Toby' won second prize in the Francis MacManus Awards for 2004 and was broadcast on RTE Radio in June 2005.

'Word-eater' won first prize in the North Tipperary Short Story Competition in 2001, second prize in the Maria Edgeworth Short Story Competition in 2001, and was published in *Writers Abú* 2000.

'Osmosis' won first prize in the Bill Naughton Short Story Competition, 1995; first prize in the Moore Literary Award, 1995; and was published in the *Mayo People* and *Splinters*.

'Dry Bones Time' won first prize in the South Tipperary Short Story Competition, 1998, and first prize in the Golden Pen Award, 1999.

'World of Trees' was shortlisted for the Fish Short Story Competition and Galway Bay FM Competition 1996, and published in *Dog Days and Other Stories*, 1997.

LICK OF THE LIZARD

I am sweeping myself into the dustbin. Every day I take the brush and run it along the wooden floor-boards honeyed by age, marked and pitted by pots dropped in moments of un-coordination. I inch it into corners, sidle it around the legs of furniture, so that when I arrive at the door, my brush has rounded up another day's gathering of myself. Little piles of dirty grey dust that cling to the sides of the plastic white bin liner. And what is it? Sloughed off skin cells. My skin cells. I cannot tell when I sweep up the bits whether it's an arm cell or a nail cell or a brain cell for that matter. I seem to gather into corners, in little puffballs that stick to the bristles of the brush which I have to comb off at the end of my sweeping, like a weaver carding wool. I am already half way towards burial.

I look at Lisa's fifteen-year-old skin, the softest, blemish free, the living bloom of youth upon her cheeks; the gloss of her black hair as it nests in around her ears, the brightness of her eyes. She walks around unaware of her beauty. That's what I don't like about her; she's too beautiful to be my daughter. She doesn't have to worry about sweeping her cells into the dustbin. Her cells are too busy still replicating and bouncing around with life force to be anxious about epidermis or collagen.

They say our cells are renewing themselves every day; that over seven years we have renewed our whole body and we're really not the same persons we were seven years before. No wonder I have a problem with Lisa. She's not the person she was two years ago. Because all her cells have been changed, I am no longer dealing with someone I can make head or tail of. Someone I can like. She was a nice little girl once. Not any more; she blames me.

When I've finished sweeping I go and make myself a cup of tea. Lisa joins me when she comes in from school; leaves her bag quietly in the corner, hangs up her coat. She's not supposed to do that. She's supposed to fling her bag where I'll fall over it, throw her coat on the chair that will eventually slither onto the floor and get walked on, so I can scream at her and tell her I am sick of the way she treats her clothes. But no. She treads gently, angel-like, her brown eyes as clear as spring water; asks me would I like a biscuit. She tells me a little about her day before she goes upstairs to do her homework.

We have been three years like this now. Ever since her father died, without a warning, leaving the two of us together without him to keep us apart. Lisa came back from basketball training one evening and found him in the kitchen slumped over the table as if he were asleep, his tea untouched, egg yolk stuck to his hair. When I returned from my night out with the girls, I found her note on the table. She was in the hospital with him. I was too late. A stroke they said. Lisa cried for days. He was an old man when I married him but not old enough to die, I would have thought. And I swear he was her father, though there's many the biddy who would have liked to claim otherwise. She had neither his looks nor any of his ways. Molly Heffernan claimed the fairies must have come and switched her when we weren't looking because we didn't put the tongs across the cradle. Maybe Molly's right, she's a little bit too smart for us all. Would mind mice at the crossroads. She doesn't say it but she walks with an air of one who keeps too much too close to her chest. I don't like that in a person. My daughter especially.

It was a while before I started to go out again. I wasn't going to be the fodder for their gossiping sodalities, or the theme for Father Toughy's Sunday sermon. A few of the smart buckos started sniffing around thinking I was easy prey now, God help their sense. Wives turned away from me at socials, put their hands possessively on their husbands' arms if I said more than hello to them. How were they to know that I wouldn't be bothered going for bacon and cabbage when I could now taste gourmet? That is why I was so pleased to see Dave.

He hadn't changed at all. At first, when I saw him in the kitchen I thought it was just someone who reminded me of him. The way he was standing there with that careless look hanging around him. I wouldn't have seen him in all this time but then he took a drag on a cigarette and I was certain. I recognised the smell- a London smell, Kilburn High Road smell, and laughed to myself when Sal Fine sniffed the air and asked who was burning tealeaves on top of the range. His brain cells must be burning up quicker than mine, I thought, though how he kept his body cells together, I couldn't understand for his hadn't aged at all. Not like mine. Still the long legs, the lean flat stomach, a rarity in men of his age, his hair still long, the beginnings of grey.

I watched that old familiar way he combed his fingers through it and I was going back to that first smell of freedom as the boat sailed out of Dun Laoghaire and headed towards Holyhead. My first summer in London. The clunk of the train as it made its way across the night to arrive in Euston all baggy eyes from a rough crossing and lack of sleep. Here was a new world of cockney accents, porters with black faces; the smell of dirt smoke. I met up with the crowd from college who were over there before me. We got work in an hotel near James' Park. One evening on my way home from a long shift skivvying, I was heading up out of the tube station. This lean body came hurrying down the steps and crashed into me and I would have tumbled back into the black hole of tunnel if he hadn't rushed out his hand and grabbed me. He insisted on bringing me back to his flat with the awful smell of gas on the air, sitting me down and running next door for two Turkish coffees that would support a spoon standing they were so black and thick. Then he took out his Rizla papers and rolled himself a smoke. It was the first time I smelled dope as he called it, the smell that was now all over Malachy Russell's kitchen.

I seldom saw my own flat after that, returning just to be there for the phone call that came as regular as the Angelus from Ireland every Friday evening. Easy Rider posters on the wall, Midnight at the Oasis playing, the hard mattress on the floor. Every morning I headed off to work in the Park Hotel, my eyes dark from lack of sleep where I bundled stained sheets into a trolley and replaced them with crisp clean ones. I renewed thin bars of soap, straightened bibles on lockers and returned in the evening to the warmth of his arms. How could I forget the evening I was cooking some dinner for the two of us when I burned my hand on the edge of the saucepan? I cried out with the pain. He just took my hand and put it to his mouth licking it all over with his tongue. He told me he had a cure for burns from the time he was eleven. There he was sitting on a rock blistering from the sun when a lizard, taking advantage of the heat, darted across and licked him. I believed him, falling more and more in love with his strong thighs, his blonde curly hair and his blue eyes. Foolishly believing he had such a cure until he slithered off and left me smouldering away without him.

So. He's here again. He had mentioned once to me about being a distant relation to Malachy's family but I had forgotten all about it until now. He doesn't recognise me at first but as the recognition dawns I can see his mind going over the last time we were together and a smile curls on his lips. We talk a little and then he asks if we can go somewhere quiet. We go out the door with his arm around my shoulder and Sal Fine's mouth as wide as the Shannon when she sees us go.

We go to a small pub in the next village. Not that it gives us much privacy. The news will be back in Malachy's kitchen before I have finished my first glass. I drink too much red wine and fall against his shoulder when we walk towards the car, laughing as I make various attempts to get into it and have to be helped. He plays John Lennon all the way home. He's still in never, never land.

I ask him in for some coffee when we get back. Lisa's still up. She's crouched over the kitchen table working on some project that has to be finished for her exam. She lifts her head.

'Hi', she says quietly.

'Lisa, this is Dave, an old friend I met at Malachy's wake. We're just having some coffee'.

'Well, I'll leave you so'. And with that she starts to fold up her books.

'What have you there?' Dave asks, 'It looks pretty complicated'.

'Not really. Just a database for an accounting firm that has to be included in this project'.

As she goes into the details of the project, I can see it happening before my eyes. Her devious little ways, her quiet voice that makes him incline his head even further to hear her explanations. When she looks up into his eyes, I can see. He is being drawn in. Then she yawns, draws back her chair and says goodnight to us.

'She's gorgeous, isn't she', he says when she has gone, 'but I'm not surprised. She'll have them crawling out of the woodwork before very long'.

'Not so sure about that. I know most mothers are supposed to think their daughters are beautiful but Lisa, she's a bit too quiet in her looks for my liking. There isn't a bit of me in her, or her father for that matter.

'Her skin's like yours was', he says, touching my cheek.

'*Was* being the operative word'.

I feel the old green-eyed monster raising its head.

'No, you still look terrific. Are you doing anything tomorrow? Maybe we could meet in town for lunch'.

'I'd love that'.

Later as I cover my face with night cream, I remember the times when I couldn't sleep for want of him and, when it was finally over, how I walked through James' Park with the trees about to turn, knowing there would never be anyone like him.

We have a great lunch. He says he's thinking of staying around for a couple of weeks. The job in London isn't that important. It can wait. It's so long since he's been home. It would be nice to be able to catch up on some old times. His questions about Matty's death are full of concern. How hard it was for me bringing up a daughter alone. He wants to know all about her. This talk soon tires me. I say it's time to go home.

We return just as Lisa is coming back from school in her maroon gym slip and grey blouse. Dave takes her bag and walks up the path with her, asking her about her day, the different teachers, things like that. She comes up to his shoulder, he leans down to her; she laughs. When we get in I pour us a drink, Dave slips into the chair by the window, crosses his legs. Lisa goes into the kitchen and starts to fry up some lunch for herself. Suddenly there's a scream from her. Dave runs into the kitchen before I even get to the door. Grease from the pan has jumped out and splashed her. Then I hear Dave saying, 'don't worry, I have a cure for that'. And I know exactly what he's going to say. I can repeat it almost word for word. How he was once a small boy that sat on a rock and a lizard licked him and gave him a cure for burns. He is saying all of this while he is looking into her soft eyes and licking her hand. She is feeling the power of him as the smoke from the pan rises up into the ceiling and the fire alarm goes off. Neither of them does anything, so I run out into the hall swatting it with the dishtowel until I can disperse the smoke. The bleeping stops.

I take up the brush and start to sweep. Now I have my cells and Lisa's all mixed up together. Dave's cells don't fall off like ours, not in little pockets to be swept into the dustpan. When he grows out of his skin it gets tighter and tighter until it splits and it sloughs off in one go. Just like the lizard that licked him.

Make My Bed and Light the Light

'This is how a bird gets to know a person', Aunt Lillis told Tess. 'It sits on your head and cleans your hair'. The weaver bird had flown in from the kitchen and landed on the young girl's shoulder. 'It picks away like it was fine-combing you for nits, but it's not that, no, not that. It gets familiar with your hair smell, the oils in the strands, the little pinholes where the hair comes out of the head. It remembers you and then it's not afraid of you any more'.

Tess's scalp remembered the way the school nurse pulled the nits from her head, the sound as she pronounced another one crunched between her nails. She waited for the bird to peck at her, but it didn't. It swayed back and forth on the raglan sleeve of her blue jumper, worrying her hair. Then it lifted and circled the room, fluttering in front of the mirror at the flamboyant impostor beyond the glass, before Aunt Lillis made a clicking maracas sound with her mouth, opened it and the bird flew to peck food from her teeth. That worried Tess even more. She was only a week in her aunt's house and already her skin was turned inside out like an old sock. She missed her mother and the smell of her.

Aunt Lillis was her mother's sister. She had a cage full of birds, mainly finches. Cordon Bleus, Weavers, Gouldiens.

'Look at their finery', she said, standing in front of the wire mesh, admiring them. The birds' colours startled the girl. 'Just look. Aren't they a picture? Lady's such a rainbow bird, better than a cockatiel or a cockatoo. She tells the world fair and square that she doesn't have to sing to shine', and putting her fingers through the cage she stroked the bright yellow head of the bird, directing her words at it as she rubbed her fingers under its throat. 'Our Tess here, now, she's no Lady Gouldien, no colour at all. Ask her where her colour is, ask her where it is'. She turned to look at her niece and in a squawking voice said. 'Where's your colour, girl, where's your colour? Did your mother wash it clear out of you, make you a standard canary, plain and ordinary with no song?

Tess wanted to cry. She didn't think she ever had any colour to wash out, except when they painted at school, bright splashes of reds and yellows and blues on the back of rolls of old wallpaper that wept from her fingers as she washed them in the cracked Belfast sink at the end of the classroom.

Tess knew her mother by her hair. She missed the smell of its unveiling, that cigarette smoke smell of it as she untwined it from its knotted plait and leaned over the sink. She rubbed shampoo into it and watched how it splayed out under water when she rinsed away the white foam that gurgled through the plug hole into the ground beneath the caravan. She had pinned a blanket around the door, stuffed papers in the windows to keep out draughts. They sat in front of the Superser while she brushed it dry. She missed the smell of it afterwards, clean and shiny, unadorned.

'You're to call this home now', Aunt Lillis said. Dark bubbling fruit spat out of the preserving pan as she put cellophane tops on jars, the room smelling of burnt sugar and quince. Birds the colour of Lucozade preened on the window sill. 'Edna should never have worn that coat. It's what addled her think-box. Wearing someone else's coat. A bird knows not to wear another's coat'.

Tess was left with no one but Aunt Lillis. Aunt and her birds. For most of her twelve years she and her mother Edna had lived in the mobile home on Aunt's land though there was a time when she remembered a flat on a third floor somewhere, looking out onto lichen on slated roofs, chimney cowls.

'Up with the pigeons', Aunt Lillis said when she came to take them away, the church clock working its giant hand around the day; voices that carried up from the street through the open window. She packed their belongings into two black sacks, her mother curled up in the bed like a shrimp, crying, her cigarette perched on the locker smoking down to ash, alone; Lillis telling her to pull herself together for the sake of the girl as she bundled them and their jetsam into her van. She brought them back to her house, sacks of sunflower seeds and peanuts on the bare concrete floor of the scullery, the air loud with chirping and squawking.

They moved into the caravan she had across one of the fields. It had a kitchen with a table that turned into a bed at night for Tess and another tiny room where her mother slept. There was a geyser that didn't work. Once a fortnight Tess was sent down to have a bath in Aunt's house. The tap's constant drip left a long slime of green down the enamel as she tried to wash herself with one arm across her breasts for fear the birds would peck at her bundles as her mother called them. The water smelled of algae.

Every other day they gave themselves a lick and a promise in the small kitchen sink of the caravan. Her mother was always happier after her hair was washed. The washing took the bad out of her head she said; that badness that had built up inside her skull bones all week, until she would moan and get Tess to tie some old tights around it just to keep it together. Other times she would send her running to the chemist for his magic cough brew. There was something in the mixture that settled her. The yellow beak of the bottle fanned out against her mouth. The brown viscous syrup ran down her chin, until it was finished. Then she felt calm, all smoothed out and slept. Sometimes after the medicine she laughed in her sleep.

Once when she woke she was still laughing. She laughed and joked and held her sides as if they would melt, become liquid. She said she was dreaming about the time Lillis had a soft spot for Tim Hyland and cycled over to his place, the narrow stems of her ankles turning the pedals as she cycled to a man because she liked the thin lips of him. He taught her how to skin a rabbit and roll her own cigarettes but left her for a woman with ten acres of arable and a short cough. Liquid, her mother's laugh, was liquid.

After that Aunt Lillis took off to America with her visa and x-rays under her arm. She stayed gone for fifteen years, buying sweepstake tickets in the hope that Lady Luck would make a call and she could buy a house in Yonkers with plastic coverings on her couch and a weeping willow in the garden. But she met a woman on Fordham Road one Sunday morning, coming back from Mass. The woman's clothes smelled of mountains and she packed her case with all the 45 records she had recorded of herself in the tiny booth at the top of the Empire State Building; singing into a magic machine above the high rise buildings. Letting her crackly, far away voice fly out over Staten Island, Manhattan, Central Park, *pack up all my cares and woe, here I go singing low, bye, bye blackbird.* The black vinyl recordings were stuffed in among her clothes and her shoes. The lid snapped shut on a dream she had for herself. When she came back, Aunt Lillis turned to birds.

Her house was far too big for Tess who had grown accustomed to the narrow living of the caravan, the familiarity of it. Here there was space but it was crowded with cages and perches and wings always stretching or flapping. She wished she could go back to the evening before her mother's apparition. That evening when the sun went down between the houses of the estate on the far side of the road and Christ's face appeared on the kitchen wall of the caravan. Her mother saw it. He was there, his sad eyes, his unkempt beard, long hair, his amorphous outline tattooed to the dingy beauty board. She called Tess in from the steps where she was sitting, drawing. All Tess saw were the splashes of tea and grease on the wall and a shadow of something looking more like a chimney pot than a countenance. Still her mother was adamant. It was His way of telling her that she could make a new life for herself and her daughter. 'It's just like the cloth of Veronica', she whispered, her eyes bright with redemption, 'the one she wiped his face with on the Via Dolorosa'.

Soon the news spread. People started coming to the caravan door. Tix and Maggie knelt on the green lino, blessed themselves and started the rosary. Annie threw holy water all around the van, sprinkling the doorways and windows. They said Edna was made for apparitions. 'She was made for miracles', they chorused as they listened to her revelations. They drank tea with her and brought plates of corned beef and egg and onion sandwiches that they ate while they watched the room darken. The sun went down between the row of houses and the face melded into the wall of the caravan.

It was there again the following evening and the next. News carried on the wind. People from outside the estate began to turn up. A local paper interviewed Edna. It quoted her saying she always knew God would find her out no matter where she hid. She would give up drinking the chemist's brew. She would leave the bottles that lined the underneath of the caravan like a roman heating system right where they were. They would be a constant reminder of her salvation. She blew a plume of cigarette smoke out the side of her mouth and picked a speck of tobacco from her tongue. To see and believe, that was the thing.

Tess sat on the steps outside and sucked the wisps of her blonde hair. Biding her time until this would be over. The interviewer was sitting at the table, her bed. She would get no sleep until they were all gone home.

When cars started parking in the field because there was no room on the road and the grass was churned up by sinking wheels, Aunt Lillis came shouting to the door. She held an apple under her sister's nose. 'You believe that because a woman took a bite out of this, took a lump out of something no better than a turnip, a potato hanging from a branch, that a man signed himself up for a crucifixion. No man'd do that. No, he wouldn't do that. Not for a bitter piece of fruit. Now if it was a mango, a hot peppery juicy mango, I'd have some believing, a mango's not ordinary, no, not ordinary. But ...'

'You're a right one to talk, letting birds peck from your teeth like a crocodile. You're a crocodile, Lillis, you just want to devour my living'.

'Are you now practicing to be a half-wit, Edna? Since the day you bought Maud Beasley's coat and put it on your back you've been like this, a coat not fit for the county home and where you'll end up if you don't cut this out'.

Tess knew about Maud Beasley. Her aunt had told her. She was taken away, her skin grey from malnutrition, hair falling out when she complained to the priest that someone was stealing the plastic dogs that came free in the cornflakes packets. Afterwards when her brother sold up the place and put all her jumble out on the street for sale, he found boxes of cornflakes uneaten, the free plastic gifts lined up in rows on the mantelpiece, the table, along the side of the bath. Edna bought her coat, a black one with an astrakhan collar. She bought four sets of the dogs, black poodles, Yorkshire terriers, border collies and Scotties that she put on the pelmet above the caravan window and let Tess draw them on days when the world disappeared into the rain running down the window.

Tess was frightened by her aunt's words. She ran from the steps to the crashed car in the ditch. Here, her mother or her aunt wouldn't find her and she would stay until Aunt Lillis left. She sat with her back against the seat, her bony knees drawn up. Now in her own place she could let her skin breathe. She took a copy from her pocket, a piece of charcoal and began to make lines on the page of what she saw from the broken windscreen of the car, the trunk and branches, the tracery of leaves on the red bonnet. That morning, she had watched her mother empty the cough bottle down the sink, heard the clink of her mother's words. It would be different this time. She said it with such belief, as she took out the new hair clip she had brought from town, brushed her hair and pinned it back from her forehead, that Tess wanted so badly to believe her. Then she could let go of the fear of twilight that settled its claws into her, willing herself to forget the sound of her mother lurching down the road, chasing the white horses that came every time her head acted up, the light fading, loneliness creeping among the hawthorn. Tess would follow her. She would find her crumpled in the ditch somewhere, asleep, bring her back to the house, roll her into bed.

She waited until she heard Aunt Lillis, singing as she went across the fields, *Make my bed and light the light, I'll be home late tonight.*

For ten days her mother revelled in the attention. He had come to her a mere sinner. She put on makeup and tied her hair in a blue ribbon. She made them breakfast. French toast with sugar that they ate at the table when Tess's bed was folded under it, the door open to the morning, letting the smoke from the pan out. Jesus had appeared to her out of his goodness. She was ready for callers, ready to sing his praises.

Until one Thursday builders came and demolished the derelict houses in the estate opposite. Tess watched the chimney stacks turning to powder when they came crumbling down, dust taking flight into the air. That evening Christ didn't show; or the next, or the next. The beauty board held only stains of tea and grease and nothing else.

Tess was cycling down the road with the last of her mother's money to buy a bottle of the chemist's brew. Later she heard her raving into the small of the night, the wafer walls of the caravan making her believe she could reach out and touch her mother's hair where it had stuck to her face after she got sick. The girl got up and pulled a jumper over her pyjamas and went and washed her as she lay there on the ground, placing her hair in the basin and sponging the sourness out of it, getting her back to bed, turning her on her side, a pillow behind her so that she couldn't roll onto her back.

The next day her mother put the scissors in the girl's hand and told her to cut. She turned away as she felt the blade snip through the lengths of hair, the sound of its falling as the blades cut through the brown strands. Afterwards her head looked too big for her body. She didn't look like her mother any more.

Tess watched her as she went out the door that afternoon, her hair spiked and dark, the water dripping off the eaves, the same motion of different rain learning from itself over and over again, dropping its berries, its jewels. She sat on the steps. Here she could hug her knees and be the best daughter she could be. The best girl in the world. She watched a rat run in and out of the wall opposite where they threw the slops from the basin, potato peelings, tea bags and grease from chips. She read about a Chinese torture once where they strapped a copper pan over the prisoner's belly and put a rat inside and heated the copper pan. The rat had only one way out.

Aunt Lillis said her mother died of an incidental. She told her that, while they waited for the ambulance to come and bring her to the hospital's mortuary. A man drove by on his moped. A goose egg on wheels, his round belly and white helmet slowed down to see what was happening, before the ambulance man moved him on. A mother out to feed the ducks with her young son let him eat the blue-moulded bread as she hurried him away, shading his eyes. Tess had found her mother sitting in the park staring into a laburnum; bird shit on her hair, covering one eye, the other staring out. Tess jumped off her bike and knelt in front of her 'Mam, it's me, Tess'.

The incidental was a clot that moved to her brain leaving her solid and dead on the park bench. Before the paramedics lifted her onto the stretcher, Tess saw how she might draw her, her elbow resting on the arm of the bench; sitting there in her pink skirt, her jumper pockmarked with little balls of pilling. But if she drew her it would be with her hair still long, separated into three strands, turning one over the other, plaited and pinned.

'You can't sit down with a bird', Aunt Lillis said as she put her leg up on the table and clipped her toenails. Little slivers of yellow keratin snapped off and flew onto the table and the floor. Tess was sitting at the other end, drawing. A piece landed on her paper.

'Unless they invite you, of course. You always have to leave it up to them. When they sit, when they fly. They were born to do that, to use their wings, to tangle the sky with their feathers. Everything else is beneath them, you know. Your mother was like them, a bit of a swift, spent her entire time in the air. Knew if she landed she could never take off again. Isn't that right, Lady?' Then she began to hum as she lifted her leg off the table, the bird at her shoulder inspecting her ear.

Walking Toby

Late at night the snakes come, slithering their way into my mind, spitting their cowardice and despair onto me until I want to scream out. I lie here in the darkness while Toby sleeps beside me, and all the devils that I have kept at bay in daylight hours break in and take up residence. Sometimes my body grows so heavy, I feel like I am a boulder in a hammock, my arms folded across my breast, my legs like steel.

On rare nights when the salamanders give me a reprieve, I could let my body soar, feel it float until it almost touches the ceiling. It stays up there until sleep takes over and I wake the next morning under the same old quilt. Toby licks my face and I scratch his turf-brown head, sniff his devoted-dog smell, as he pushes his nose into the crook of my arm. His eyes look at me as if to say, 'don't go to the hospital today; take me for a walk instead, down by the pier. I can bark at the seagulls, you can watch the boats feather their way across the bay as you drink from your flask of tea: pack Chewies for me'.

Instead he watches me get dressed; sit into Mrs. Pearson's car that takes me to the day ward. It is where we women meet, every second Thursday, sitting in our padded chairs, telling the nurse whether we want coffee or tea, brought to us on lap-trays painted with sunflowers. Outside, the day pours down on the ivy that covers the building opposite, on the world working itself into a frenzy. In here we are sheltered from all of that by the bright, cheery curtains, pictures on the walls of serene countryside, Lyric FM soothing us with Albinoni.

The chat flies across the room. How we've all been since the last time we met. We, the Thursday women. How well we look, the colour of our hair, so good, so real. This could be the hairdresser's and we are getting beautified for an outing to the races or a nephew's wedding, where we'll make sure we're looking our best. They all tell me mine's a perfect match; that unless you were told, you wouldn't know the difference. I press the remote control of my chair; raise my feet a little so that I can ease the pain in them. My hair. It was the one thing I loved most about me, you know. My lovely hair. There is a new batch of magazines for us to read.

Mary stretches in her chair, claiming it as hers for these hours. She has been up since six, travelling the cruel roads from Glenamaddy to get her here on time. 'These chairs are as valuable as the best seats in Carnegie Hall for a Pavarotti concert', she says to us, as she stretches again. She is grateful, knowing that if she didn't get her spot today, she could be looking at the huge overwhelming fear of being left another week. But sitting in her chair, the vein found, she can relax with the *Reader's Digest* DIY manual. It's her book, we say. She is probably the only one ever to pick it from the coffee table that holds the yellow plastic boxes of cotton wool and sharps. This Thursday she wants to know how to fix the leaking cistern in her toilet. Drip, drip, it goes, all night long. Mary tries to fix everything. Up until this happened, she had been trying to fix the people in her life. First her aunt with Alzheimer's, then her father, a quiet man, who collapsed in a ditch on the long road from the pub. When they found him next morning his face was frozen into the heather. Little twigs were stuck to his skin when they turned him over.

Her mother had been dead for years. All this dying in a house that was so remote even the home help stopped coming to her across the mountain road that was potholed and forgotten. The few neighbours who took the time to visit her after she had buried her father, kept telling her that her tiredness was due to the hard time she was after having, and told her to get herself some cod liver oil tablets. But somewhere inside her she knew it wasn't that. 'Drip, it goes all night long', she says, 'that feckin' cistern, drip, drip, take the ball-cock out, replace it with a new one, so simple, gillie gillie, just like that the book says'.

Drip, drip, the saline goes in, little salt pearls that flow gently along the vein with no noise at all. It's the same with the glucose, same with my fix, my concoction that comes in its episcopal purple covering. The nurse arrives covered in her riot gear, blue plastic apron, blue gloves, blue, blue mask across her mouth. She carries my bag at arm's length, attaches it to the array of wires on the long steel stand I'm plugged into. 'If I could sing, I'd be a stereo', I tell them. Roisín laughs.

Mary is going to build a cover for her radiator when all this is over. She's going to make it herself from cream MDF. It shows her how to do it in the book. Shiny brass mesh to hide the ugliness. She's going to give the house a real going over as well. She may even get a grant for a shower. One with a seat attached to the wall, that flips down, so that she can sit when her legs don't seem to hold her very well. She keeps going back to this DIY book. 'Maybe the book will tell me how to plug myself in at home', she says. 'Then I could be fixing the drip while the drip is fixing me'. Mary never gives up. She could wish for the cloth of heaven to come down and heal her but she doesn't wait for it. Instead, she comes like us on these Thursdays to have our veins, now parchment thin, searched out like lugworms in the sand, which sends the pain shooting to the stars.

I think about my hair, my beautiful hair. 'Such healthy, healthy hair', people used to say. The way it curled around my ears, softening my face. I didn't need to do anything with it, just let it be. Then watching it fall, come out in fistfuls in the shower, on the comb, a nest of it on the pillow in the morning, my forehead growing higher and higher like Elizabeth the first.

At night when I cannot face the dark for fear of what it might bring, I stand by the window and look down at the garden. Shadows hover in corners and I wonder if I will get to plant the tulip bulbs that I bought in Woodies one day in a flicker of hope. I remember the night I saw a movement beyond the cotoneaster, low to the ground, barely moving. I went down and found a dog crouched against the shed's wall. I went to rub him and he growled a belly-threatening growl, his teeth bared, the fur on his neck standing. His ears were blood encrusted and bare skin showed through where the remnants of a rope had held him. He had been through the wars, a bit like me. He was all bones and neglect. His growl told me clearly what he thought of humans. I brought him down some water, some rasher rinds left from my tea. I placed them a few feet in front of him so that he had to snake his way along the ground to gobble them. Another piece was placed a little further on and I continued to do that until he had worked his way into the coalshed by the house. Then I left him there to sleep on an old coat.

He was there the next morning with eyes that said 'come near me and you'll be minus a hand', so I improvised. I attached a woollen glove to the handle of the sweeping brush and three or four times a day went down and sat on the old deckchair in front of Toby. With my extended arm I rubbed his back with the glove, letting the softness touch him; shortening my distance every other day until the glove and my hand were equidistant. Then I slipped my hand into the glove and stroked him. The day he licked my glove was the turning point. He will be waiting for me when I return today.

I find my buzzer and press it. Me and my drip need to be unplugged from the wall before I can move out of my seat. 'I want to take my dog for a walk', I say to the nurse who comes to unplug the stand that holds my fix. She helps me into my slippers, steadies me as I hold onto the steel bar of the stand. For now this can be Toby and the only walk we will take today. Then I take myself and my tall steel lanky dog in its purple coat down the corridor to the toilet. I pull him along, obedient, well used to his walk now, able to side-step other women with their own dogs with different coloured coats.

Toby doesn't make a sound as Mandy walks by with her steel dog, Mandy in her blue jeans and tight tea-shirt, a ring in her nose, a baseball-cap. She hasn't gone for the wig like us older women. She didn't wait for her hair to be left on the pillow every morning, to look in the mirror and say, who is this woman looking back with hair as thinned as a witch from Macbeth, no eyebrows, no eyelashes? When she saw the first fistful on her comb, she just shaved it all off. Found a baseball cap that said *vive la difference* and thought no more of it. She says that her son plays with her wig at home. She gave it to him for his Airfix soldiers. A safe bunker for them in the camouflage of auburn tresses. She seems to take it in her stride; doesn't let fear gather in every new pain.

The nurse comes and takes our trays. I pick up one of the magazines. The Royals make the front cover. Again. Inside Helen Mirren tells me that stripping off gets easier as you get older. I read it out to the other women, they laugh.

'I've found that too', Mary says. 'I do it all the time. Once you've done it for one consultant, you can do it for them all. Their hands checking my scar, searching, mapping out my body like a cartographer'.

I study the beauty of her when she played Caesonia to Malcolm McDowell's Emperor, envy the beauty of her now. Maybe I should have been more daring, taken all those chances which I never did. Then I could sing *'Je ne regrette rien'* and mean it, really mean it.

Roisín is reading *Who Wants to be a Millionaire*. She's not wasting her time. She's planning to have brushed up on all her general knowledge before her treatment is finished. She plans to get on the television programme. She plans to win. She shouts the questions across to us:

For two hundred euro - where is the river Seine?

For four hundred euro - what is a collection of sheep called?

And the million euro question is ...?

But none of us wants to ask that. How can we? We could call on the audience for its help, but there's no one here. Maybe I'll phone my friend. Toby, are you there, Toby? Sorry your friend doesn't know the answer either. What's left then but to go fifty: fifty? Well, I suppose it's as good a chance as any.

Word-Eater

'Newspapers', the woman with the small head cried, 'are what she has done to me. The smell of them, their inks and sizings, their groundwood pulp. The smell of tabloids, broadsheets, of editorials, the ink of the financial page, of gossip columns. She smells of them, my sister, all those pages breathing out their fumes onto me, so that it clings to me like a bad body odour. I have grown to hate that smell, the way her room is choked with it. A room that has no corners but those that the towers of papers have created. Sometimes I lock her in her room, hoping that she will be absorbed into the newsprint and I'll never have to open the door again. Then the smell won't come slinking down the stairs and fill my living space. I wish', she whispers, 'I could put her in the pulping machine with a pile of her papers, see her go through the washers, the headbox, see her ground until the fibres soften, lignin and inks mixed up with her tissues'.

This woman stops talking, her face suddenly takes on the aura of serenity. No one would think that a head so small could store such hate towards her own sister, a little old woman somewhere who doesn't know that her actions can raise such invective, such cruel valediction. Small-headed woman looks up into Word-eater's eyes; she has spoken the unspeakable, said what she has been thinking for so long; secure in the knowledge that the dumb woman before her will say nothing, knows that she has taken it all in, never to breathe the word to a soul. In the end was the word and the word was eaten.

Before she leaves, she places a blue plastic bag on the table. She has brought Word-eater enough to feed her for a week.

Which is good because the next person might bring her something that is of no value at all, like a CD player or a pair of Hush Puppies. This blue bag holds tins of tuna, a loaf of bread, spaghetti hoops and kiwis. By the time small-headed woman has reached the bottom of the hill, Word-eater has torn out the white belly of the bread and started to eat it.

They come from all over, these people. They have a path worn up to her house since they discovered her. She is amazed how there are so many people who need to tell their secrets to someone who is neither priest nor psychiatrist; how they don't want to have to be in their coffins before a sin eater is called to eat a plateful of their human frailties. Word-eater goes beyond that, she eats their words, whatever they spoon her, sad or glad. They know she will offer no advice, no solution, no absolution because she cannot and anyway that is not what they want. They walk up the path - Yanks, English, French - weighed down by the crucifixion of their anger, their rosaries of regret, arriving at the most unearthly hour.

One night she was just settling in, about to pull the blinds on the rain clattering the roof like a bitch, when she saw a light coming up the path. A firefly dancing in the blackness of the driving rain. Not an iota of light anywhere but from the little lamp attached to the band across the head. She listened for the knock that came four times before she opened wide and beckoned this firefly to come in.

He was Japanese. He stood like a stork, about to remove his shoes but she motioned him to stop. Her floor was far too cold for that. He sat in front of her as they all do. Laid his offering down, a camera, a great big thing with automatic focussing, snazzy case. Maybe he thought she could use it sometime; walk along the cliff, take the birds gliding across the blue, a close-up of sea holly, its silver mauveness shimmering in the light. He started talking, in the rhythmic even beat of his own language, and though Word-eater didn't understand a syllable, she had a good idea by the inflected words that he was speaking of a great sadness. She had become a reader of faces, and knew as his expressions changed that he had reached the deep down hurting parts, his wife unfaithful perhaps, he himself dishonest in his love, the secrets he could tell to no one else because they would be gossiped over a cup of green tea, a sake. It must have been a great suffering for him to come half way across the world to tell it to her as she sat like a Zen Buddhist doing zazen. He continued to talk until his face began to brighten; then he got up, bowed and went out the door carrying lightness.

She studied his gift; a lightproof box that could have captured an instant of his unease, the slow development of his brightening. That day she was his camera, opened briefly the shutter behind his grief, let it be exposed so that she could get an image in her mind even if she couldn't understand a word.

They come. Perhaps it's a mother angry with her daughter who should have long broken free from home, who just swans around the house all day admiring her adamantine features in the mirror, files her nails, asks her mother to iron her linen shirt before she goes out. This mother knows if she seeks another expert, she will be given advice. She will be told that she should look at her back because she has door-mat written all over it, that what her daughter needs is a good kick up the arse. But the mother doesn't want to hear this; she needs to have a reason for getting up in the morning, and without her daughter she doesn't have that. Without her she might have to look at her own life. So she comes. And she talks. Word-eater takes in each syllable, each noun, pronoun, each sweet cadence and assimilates it into her; each linking verb, each hard consonant, soft vowel. She eats her words like there is no tomorrow, as if her life depended on it. She takes them all in, swallows them and digests them. She grows fat on them.

It doesn't matter what they tell her, she won't gag on their horror, of people they have mutilated, buried under garden fountains, of mouths grown crooked from holding a whiskey bottle in it too long; of rats that come and eat their toes when they are out of it with drink, verse after verse of terror. But it is not all sadness. She eat happy words too, stories that would make a person cry with joy; of babies born to women who have no wombs. Of men finding hope in the breasts of a young girl when they believed that all hope was lost. She takes them in like basil on sweet tomatoes, like peaches dripping juice from a southern Spanish market, like Chardonnay. These words are especially flavoursome to her. They keep her going.

Sometimes they come because they are so lonely. Once an old man came, 'just to cry', he said. He was tired weeping on his own with only the dog to look at the tears rolling onto his vest, soaking it. He loved his dog but he wanted some other human being to witness his sadness, to verify his tears for him, to prove that he was not just imagining the salt as it dried on his cheeks. But he didn't want anyone with her soothing sibilance, her 'there, there, everything will be all right' words. He just wanted someone to see.

She was chosen at birth. 'She's the one', the spirits said, as her mother pushed her out into the world in a sluice of blood water. The spirits collected all around her, whispering in the atmosphere above her. 'She's the one, the one to reclaim all the words that are spat out in anger, that are choked out in resentment. She's the one to take them all back again, all those diphthongs, dactyls, those sweet iambs of love, the caesura of a bitter word'.

They chose her from her sisters and brothers to carry out the task that had been in past generations of her family. From the time she created her first two syllables, they stifled them in her. They took her to the place with the ring of stones, where the trees crouched like a panther. They stood around her, the spirits overhead, while the elder of the family turned her upside down and washed her in vinegar; put the dark band of silence around her mouth. Then he read slowly from the Word-eater's book, eating each rice paper page as he went along, the silence growing longer and longer between each paragraph until, in the end, there was silence. Silence but for the soughing of the beech trees and the flick of her eyelashes that rushed against her cheeks.

This was her epiphany. The manifestation of her vocation that would see her tongue muscles perish, her larynx become impotent. People have learned that the most that will ever come out of her is a croak like some ugly bird, her hands holding her throat in order to force the sound out. They know they can trust her, that they won't find her standing up at a tribunal telling all and sundry what she was told on a dark evening. She will hold the story to herself. She is there to cleanse the confessor of the story that's eating him up. Who can he tell but her about his coveting. An amazing word, covet, a word that sounds like a sleek car, a fleet of ships, a noble word, for something that is a slinky mean action leaving the guilty one excited and guilty all at once - such a kind word for wanting it off with your best friend's wife. She sits and offers listening in the absence of her tongue, the folding of one hand over the other, the understanding smile. They bring her stories of a loved one that is not loved any more, that is too fat, too thin, too small, that doesn't peel an orange the way they would like them to. And afterwards they don't have to say affirmations, bring their inner child on a trip to Disneyland. They don't have to print their thanksgiving in the evening newspaper. No, nothing like that. They can remain forever victims, bullies. They come to her, then go down the hill singing.

She listens to the woman who believes she was a cat in her last life. She had a sister then. 'We were two kittens inseparable', she says, her amber eyes brimming, 'curled together as one, like two halves of a walnut in the strong shell of our seagrass basket, clung low to the ground for the same tom, ate catnip till we were drunk. Nimbus was killed by the hard rubber of a wheel that churled over gravel on a night in November. I was left alone, one half of a walnut, one whole side left open for wind and pain, lived out my days alone until the vet put me down. Now that I've come back, I miss her so much'.

A woman alone in search of a cat-sister. She doesn't advise her to forget the cat; to contact it, to meditate on it. She can come to her any time and talk to her of herself and Nimbus.

And when she has gone, gone light-weight into the dark, Word-eater stands at the window until she is nothing but a white dot of fake fur way down at end of the hill that heads onto the main road. She takes her gift of mice that she has left at the door, bites off one of their heads; leaves the rest of them while she goes to her desk. She loves chocolate. She takes out her hardback copy with a picture of hot air balloons on it; picks up her pen, begins. She writes it all down, all those beautiful eaten words, pages and pages of despair and resentment and forgiveness. She turns them, reshapes them, all silence except for the sound of the pen. She creates haiku, sonnets, villanelles. She imagines the woman, sees her following the sun around the garden, her pupils narrow in the light, finding out the spots that hold heat like a furnace, on black plastic, limestone, wood chips.

Gift of Mouth

Clara was moving out of her skin. She saw the crane lift the gibbous moon into the sky over the old town and she thought, 'this feeling, it's not like peeling away an onion, layer after dried layer, no, not like an onion nor like a gecko either, shedding off its old skin in one go'. It was more like she had a book in her belly and page after page was being torn out. The thing was she had to strip away all the pages that didn't serve her any more; chapter eleven that had a list of acquaintances from her past masquerading as confidantes, songs on page fifty seven that she had no heart for, food that she no longer had taste for; all those chapters with Gerald. Yes, Gerald too. They would all have to go, unless she could find another way.

The air was so hot she could hardly breathe. But the cats didn't mind. They stretched their liquid bodies onto the white walls of the night as they walked up the cobbled steps where the gypsies sat in the dark of their kitchens, a fan swirling the same sweltering air around and around their cigarette smoke, thinking the darkness inside could compensate for the moon in the sky. Gerald stopped at a stall to look at some leather belts. Around them beautiful people carried themselves as if their very centre knew that they being small didn't serve the world. They stepped down the cobbles steps in front of Clara, stopping in shops that sold clothes for people who believed in themselves. And someone was playing Caruso from a third floor balcony. She stopped to listen. It is what she needed, music that went deep into the centre of her. Music with balls. She wanted that, just like she wanted to sink her mouth into the sticky juice of a Claudia plum she had seen at the market earlier that day, eat it bit by bit, let its juice flow down her, until it was all gone and know that she had tasted, really tasted it. Like she could taste Gerald if he ever wanted her again. If he did he would be able to read into her belly and know that she was as thirsty as an octopus for a man who would make her sing from the middle of her book, make her sing like Caruso.

She had coaxed him to come away with her hoping that the sun and the way the heat spread out from the soles of their feet into the unforgiving cement of the footpaths would somehow bring back the feeling that they were still alive to one another. She had also heard the stories; about the good doctor, the gifts that he had, how he could change things. She wanted to find out the truth of them, if any.

They had booked into the bleached white apartments with burnt-earth roofs and rooms so clean that their cleanliness didn't even allow them the intimacy of a complaint between them. They ate by day in the small tapas bars by the pool and at night down by the harbour where the wind whipped up the tablecloths and a fat seagull walked in and around the tables pecking the bits and pieces from the ground. They spoke little. The smell of the sea came along the waterfront and there were boats. Beautiful vessels whose sails flapped against masts and where laughter rose from cabins. That night they had walked to the old town as the moon rose. On their way back they stopped at the gate to look at a statue of a crouching man made from rough terracotta clay. Gerald went to take a photograph of it and the eyes opened a startling white against the red earth. Gerald threw him two euro and terracotta man closed his eyes again. They walked back, he in front of her, his hands in his pockets.

A quintet were playing on the small dance floor beside the pool when they got back to the complex. Clara, sitting on the low wall that surrounded the dance floor was glad of the breeze that ruffled the tamarinds. Three couples moved around the floor under the light of the moon while Abdullah brought fresh drinks to their tables. The lead singer was singing The Girl from Ipanema. She watched one man lead his partner into the easy tempo of a waltz, his hand to the small of her back. Clara could imagine the heat from his fingers blazing through the fabric of her dress as she leaned to the clean scent of his body. Cats sauntered out of darkness. She knew by the time she went back to the apartment, Gerald would be stretched out on the narrow bed, a towel covering the pillow to absorb the sweat of his hair. He had stopped loving her the year before.

She remembered the soft understanding there was between them during their first years together. How they remained intimate with one another through worry and lean times. But as they became more secure with life they loosened from each other. They unlearned what it was like to be held. There were no children.

Later she walked back to their room past the pool where a couple as old as Gerald and herself had jumped fully clothed into it and were mock tangoing around the shallow end. *'Tall and tan and young and lovely'*, they crooned to one another. Her skin longed to drink the whole thing dry.

All week she listened to the women as they lay on their sun loungers around the pool, their bodies golden, basted; sipping drinks that Abdullah, with his big smile and his snake tattoo, brought them. Gerald was sitting in the bar with some men who had just arrived having driven over the Pyrenees. One of them hung a towel over his head and went to sleep. The other latched onto Gerald and she could see his face brighten with distraction. The women were still talking, they were talking. They all had their own stories; of men in love with their wives again. How they would take their small boots in their hands, unfasten the laces and rub their tired feet for them when they came in from the long day of the field. Men who took off their own shirts still warmed by their bodies and put life into the cold shivering one, of running their hands through their wives hair until they became soft with longing. The good doctor had done this for them.

But there were the other stories too. Of the woman called Agnes Hiller who paid him one visit and left by his fire escape afraid to face anyone because of the change they would see in her. She walked out never looking back, leaving her children with her mother and her husband's dinner on a plate over a steaming pot of water. Someone told of the woman who after a few visits to the doctor drove her lover to the country market. There among the farmers selling free range pork, barrels of olive oil, curd cheese, she bartered him for a skulk of foxes. The fox woman had a way of keeping a man and the new owner of the foxes took them into her own place where they sat by the fire while she brushed their blazing red coats.

There was the woman who walked out of the doctor's surgery up into the mountain and became a hermit. She built a house up there, a little house of her own where she stayed quiet for a time. She kept goats that wandered over the massif, the sun an aureole in the sky and when she was hot and thirsty she lay down and drank milk from their udders.

Women with barren bellies climbed up the jagged rocks to see her and she plunged her hand into the well of the mountain and pulled out a red dripping baby. She baptised them there before the women left, slip-sliding down the massif to the old women in their black shawls spitting into the red earth of the market square till it turned to blood and they knew that a baby was born.

These stories stopped when one of the women climbed into the pool and the conversation turned to the variety show some of them had seen the night before with its Shirley Bassey drag queen; all huge breasts and skinny ankles, screeching out that she was simply the best, as she took an albino snake from a basket and wound it round one of the woman's shoulders. 'How cold it was', she said, an ice cold scarf that cooled the redness of her sunburnt neck.

Clara wrote the directions they gave her on the back of her hand. Next afternoon, while Gerald was drinking with his new friends in Abdullah's bar, she walked into the old town through streets with shutters closed for siesta time. She walked by the Square where a dog sat between two old men in the shade of a jacaranda tree. She walked down narrow streets to the place where the fountain was.

There were already women waiting for the heavy wooden door to open. They stood smoking and chatting, at ease, touching each other with familiarity. She watched others walk along the street, stop and greet by name some of the women already there. Clara stood apart from them. They didn't ignore her and they didn't speak with her either, but even in the different languages she could make out his name.

They were drawn to him, the women at the pool had told her, from all sorts of places, from high rise apartments to those who lived in caves in the Barranco. Some came out of curiosity when they heard the stories. Some conjured up ailments so that they could come; ailments that for years they had put up with. Backache, unexplained headaches, restless legs. Legs that did the work of legs by day but when they were stretched out at night on the cool sheets they started to jig and jump as if they wanted to run away, far away, out of the bed and down the street, rather than stay between covers that no longer warmed them. It held them from sleep and just when they thought they had silenced them and were drifting into it, their legs gave one jerk and they were wide awake and restless all over again. They heard the doctor was good for that. Of keeping women's hearts in the one place. Word had spread from village to village, town to town, across continents; how he was able to help them to go back to the stale wine of their marriages where they could find just enough flavour in them to slake their thirst until they came back to him the following year. And it did that. It kept them going.

Stories either good or bad, they were her only chance. To kill or cure, she laughed to herself. But she would have come anyway because one of the woman at the pool had described his eyes. Their generosity. She knew by the sound of them that he would help her.

The women were checking their watches. They had grown quiet with anxiety. The town clock struck and then the door opened. She moved with the others into the waiting room. They sat. A fan whirled around the ceiling giving little reprive from the heavy air. She sat staring at its brass helicopter blades and if she crossed her eyes she could see a circle inscribed on the air, its brown radius swirling around like some mathematical problem waiting to be solved. She sat. The doctor came to the door and called the woman with a large frown. She stood, growing in importance as she followed him into the room. She was the chosen one, the one not forsaken. The others crossed their legs and uncrossed them. They folded their arms, they looked at their nails. One woman counted changed in her purse. The fly on the window buzzed itself to sleep in the dust that fell silently through the air.

Clara closed her eyes and waited. She strained to hear any little sound from the doctor's surgery, getting restless when the woman with the frown didn't appear. She could hear little muffles, a soft interchange, a name maybe, a symptom, blurred. What did she expect? Loud exchanges, a scream. She would rush to the door to find bodies lying open. There would be police tape cordoning the building; sirens blazing; police cars half parked up on the footpath against the side of the building; people stretching their necks to see what was happening; pictures in the tabloids. She started to shift in her seat.

The frowning woman came out. Except the frown was gone. She turned to them clear-eyed before she went out the door putting the white script into her bag. The afternoon passed. Women came and went until he finally called Clara's name. She followed him into the surgery. He sat behind his desk and looked at her.

He asked her what books she read? 'Mainly ordinary, the banal', she said, to keep herself from dreaming. Of what? Of what it could be like if she didn't live the life she lived now. And why did she come to him? Because she heard the women talking.

Then he asked her again and she told him about the book in her belly that brought with it a great thirst.

'Every morning I wake up with the thirst of a kiss, like someone in the night rubbed salt on my lips and I cannot reach the glass of water on the bedside locker. Every morning it's the same, that same unquenchable want in me that won't go away. If you do not help me I will die of thirst. For even if I drink the rivers dry it will not satisfy me'.

'Your life will change. You may never be able to live again the way you want to'.

'That doesn't matter. I will live whatever way I will live it. There is no other'.

He came to where she was sitting on the chair and put his hands under her elbows and brought her to standing. Then he lifted up her chin and she could see his nose hairs, smell the astringent smell of antiseptic soap. She closed her eyes.

Afterwards she walked along back streets that she didn't know existed in the town. She walked down the metal stairs out onto an unfamiliar back street through cardboard boxes piled high with the smell of rotting fruit, stale urine. She sidestepped the pair of runners neatly placed beside a pair of pink high heel shoes, a pair of socks rolled up in them, a couple settling their clothes before going into their cardboard bed. She walked by the woman sweeping butterflies from her path. She walked feeling the soft bruise of her lips where he had kissed her. She grew into the walk and became quiet, her body filling up. So this is how they did it. How they stayed inside their own skin, how they sang from the middle of their books when all they could read day after day were empty covers. It was why they came year after year. A way to keep themselves going; a way to hold on. It lasted well into the winter for them, kept their marriages together, and they were grateful for that. Clara felt the pages turning in her belly. She felt herself move within her skin.

She found herself down at the sea. There were three sailboats on the horizon, as perfect as if they were painted there. A hangglider hung from the blue. A man was lining out loungers in neat rows along the stretch of sand as she walked back towards the apartment. Salt had dried into the crucible of rock where the sea lifted itself up out of the deep, before it broke across the rocks. She could taste the whole generous gift of his tongue, the little bit of hard skin on his bottom lip. She felt an energy shoot through her like a jet of water streaming down a mountain.

Meal of Small Buttons

Lorrie and Cecile like to arrive at the dining room before the clatter of cutlery and the jabber of people coming in off the golf course drown out the quartet playing softly near the bar. The waiter bows and with his hand indicates their table for the evening. It is the same table they have had since they arrived at the hotel three weeks before; in front of the window that frames the hills, the hydrangeas heading into change. Their seats are especially arranged so that they can sit close to one another, looking out into the room. Cecile likes to watch the evening diners stroll in; the Murrays predictably first, Mr. Murray smoothing down the brown rat of hair stretched across his bald patch, Mrs. Murray scanning the room with her frightened eyes as if some diner might find her out. Of what, even she can't tell. Mrs. Pinchbeck with her Shih Tsu under her arm. The Lynch's with their precocious three year old (for the hotel welcomes dogs and children). The evening sun going down in its regular place comes through the glass and warms their backs.

Lorrie waits until Cecile is seated before she tucks herself into the chair beside her. The waiter thwacks the cone of starched napkin into a square and places it on each of the women's laps, pours them some iced water. Little mauve stars float on its surface. Cecile takes the ice from the glass and chews it as she always does. It makes Lorrie smile. They have been coming to the hotel for the last ten years; leaving the city before the crazy take-over of summer tourists, where there is no redemption even in the parks, the grass covered with bodies, pink and peeling whenever rain gives way to sun; before the traffic halts on Nassau Street. They find it difficult getting used to people thronging the pavements. Here they are just far enough out of the city to make them feel at home and away at the same time. They come for the air.

'You know, my dear Lorrie, we will have to say hello to Mrs. Pinchbeck. It was so good of her to return my purse'.

'But we'll have to be civil to that bloody dog of hers, and you know I cannot bear that. It was probably the dog that stole it in the first place. I don't know which is worse, Bubbles or the Lynch's little terror. Look at him, he's already tearing the bread rolls apart'.

'Don't upset yourself, Lorrie, or there's no point in us being here at all'.

The waiter comes to take their order. There is still heat in the day. Lorrie sips her water and smiles at the Murrays who have been given a table close to the kitchen. The waiter returns with a single plate of Parma ham and places it between the two women. They take up their forks and proceed to eat, taking their time. The waiter knows to give them ten minutes before he brings them the main course. They like to sit and relish the taste before the plate of grilled chicken with orange arrives and replaces the empty one. The chicken has been cut to bite-size pieces so that they can eat without fussing. They place the pieces of meat in their mouths, chewing each piece slowly until the plate is cleared. Mrs. Pinchbeck's dog starts to howl as they finish the bowl of *creme bruleé* between them. Lorrie licks it clean with her fingers then wipes them on her napkin. Because of the fuss the dog is making, they refuse coffee.

Mrs. Pinchbeck is so distracted trying to get the table cloth out of Bubbles' mouth that she doesn't see them pull back their chairs and wander out through the French doors to the veranda, out among the bottle brush and the sumach now turning. The two women hold onto one another, and arm in arm they start their after-dinner walk down the cobble path by the serpentine pond in the direction of the clubhouse. Lorrie watches for branches that stick out and might harm Cecile, holding on for fear the wind might shake her or the bird that flies out of a bush startle her. Precious, needing minding. Hers.

As small girls, Lorrie and Cecile were inseparable. Curled together as one, Lorrie lay her head on Cecile's lap and let her rub her forehead, rub her nose against hers and give her little Cecile kisses. Only nine months between them and Lorrie has forgotten how short and brown her own hair was and how Cecile's was so fair and wavy. She only remembers their house on Dartmouth Square as crumbling. The steps up to the front door froze in winter and the leaning kitchen wall was held up by a tree trunk that their father took home from his saw mills because he never got around to fixing it. The third stair from the top landing had also rotted away. It became a game to them on their way to bed at night to see who could jump over it without letting the next step creak. Otherwise they would be dragged into the darkness. Safe in bed they curled like kittens into one another.

Somewhere off on a far green a lawnmower cuts grass. Golfers are coming in off the eighteenth hole, carting mud and their bags behind them. All they see are two middle- aged women strolling in the fading light, their arms around one another. People don't need to know and she has forgotten anyway Lorrie tells herself, but she lets out a sigh as soft as white fur collars. Cecile catches the sigh and turns to rub the fine knit of her cardigan.

'You mustn't be melancholy, my dear. You mustn't go back too far'.

'I know, I am grateful for all I have been blessed with'.

'Put time's gathering over it. Just think if the shell hadn't been broken, the bird would never have emerged'.

'You're so right. A little time and I'll have it all behind me again. And it was another life'.

In that other life Lorrie and Cecile moved with grace into it. Men eyed them at dances wondering if they would ever get close enough to choose between them as they stood laughing and self-contained in their dresses of brightly coloured overskirts. They discovered wine in the bars and cafés around the city where they went at night to listen to the music. They fed from a single plate of ravioli swimming in cheese sauce like small buttons that they forked into their hungry mouths. Sometimes they slept with the same men, going back to their bedsits off Parnell Square where everything reeked of fried onions and lamb chops. Their parents had parties for them for their coming of age. The record player filled the room with 'take these chains from my heart', while they kissed the men with pure intent against the leaning wall of the kitchen.

Their father's saw mill started to make money. There was enough to take his family to a hotel on the edge of the Atlantic with its antique floor tiles. They played backgammon in the residents' lounge, ate scones by the spitting log fire.

That holiday, the two young women took the green road along the edge of the cliffs. White feathers of foam broke the crust of land as seabirds glided past. Cecile ran along the grass and raised her arms. 'I am Cecile', she cried, 'growing up in this land of mean sun, my wings won't ever melt', and spreading them out she ran towards the spray that came up to drench her, 'I am Cecile ...' she commanded as it came up again and drowned out her voice. Lorrie stood, happy just to be watching her. If she believed she could fly, she could fly. When the next white wave had retreated, Lorrie looked up expecting to see her sister floating over her head, but the space above was just grey cloud; the cliff edge was empty. Cecile had disappeared. Lorrie ran to the edge, calling out to the foam, 'Cecile, Cecile', but all she could see was the white boiling against the rock.

'Good girl, good girl, you did the right thing', her father said when she came screaming and shivering into the foyer of the hotel and waiters and kitchen staff came running from all directions. Locals gathered in the driveway, and even though they shook their heads in memory, were still willing to search into the night. The lifeboat was called out. Divers. Months later a scarf with kingfishers was found wrapped to the neck of some serrated wreck washed up on a lower beach.

'You did the right thing', her parents repeated, over and over again, in the months that followed as they tried to hold onto the one girl they had left, grateful that she hadn't gone too, their first born. They could not pull her out of it. She stopped taking the tranquillisers the doctor prescribed. With them she couldn't feel that Cecile was gone and that was worse than anything because that left her hovering somewhere in the unknown instead of letting the tears roll down her face onto her cardigan. Friends called by, tried to console her, to wrap her in their arms and say it was alright, but when they couldn't break through, they stopped calling.

Lorrie took to going for walks along the streets on her own, along Northbrook Road, down into Ranelagh, across to Rathmines, only stopping to stare at broken things; doorways, windows splintered, gutters cracked and leaking down. Until one day she saw a man standing on Portobello Bridge. The sun shadowed a tattoo of leaf onto his left arm. She watched as he lifted his arm to push back his hair from his eyes. The shadow disappeared. When he lowered his arm again, the leaf returned.

She decided to go back to the old café where they used to spend their evenings drinking coffee, sip their first margaritas. But it had disappeared, replaced in her lost time by an Internet Café. She walked until she found another one on another street, ordered a meal of small buttons for herself. One fork idled on the opposite side of the plate while she picked up her own and began to eat.

Days fell into one another, weeks, years. Lorrie lived through her father's and her mother's deaths. She was left with only things, the house, the saw mill and Cecile's share of the inheritance. She grew into eating alone.

One day she went to a restaurant off Exchequer Street and was given a table near the window. It looked across the street into another window with wooden horizontal blinds. Through the slits she could see a pair of hands, nothing more, as if they were living on their own. The left one moved across and began to paint the nails of the right. Then the process was reversed. She couldn't make out the shade, but she could follow the movements of the brush, sweeping colour from cuticle to tip. Then the two hands were held up for inspection. A light was switched off.

A few minutes later the front door opened. The hands came out attached to their owner who fanned her painted nails in the air like a bird knowing it could fly. Then the woman walked down the street, away from the restaurant window. Lorrie's eyes followed the click of the high boots and too short skirt, to the edge of the street where she went into the baker's on the corner. The woman came out eating what she had bought and walked back again picking the crumbs from her palm. She stopped at the window and looked into the restaurant. Lorrie looked back at her; wanting to see something beyond the crouch of her shoulders, the wariness in her eyes. She nodded to the empty seat beside her. The woman pushed open the door, walked as far as her, sat and picked up the fork. She speared it into the mushrooms and finished her half without speaking. Then she stood up and left. Lorrie's eye held her in her sight till she went in the door opposite. The light went on again and shone through the horizontal blinds. She saw hands join, pray. Lorrie walked home through the back streets with trees that dropped their flowers over into the canal. She went to the wardrobe that once belonged to her sister; she took out skirts, cardigans, spread them on the bed, curled into them and slept.

She watched for the woman each time she went to the restaurant. She knew the days she was hungry because she would then be there before her. There were days she knew not to ask about the bruise on her cheek. Once before they had finished, a small thin man in a grey coat came and stood at the door. When the woman saw him, her fork scraped off the plate; she let it fall with a clatter and headed out the door with him. Lorrie didn't see her for weeks.

When she finally returned she was pale and there was a ridge of dark under her eyes.

'Why do you let him do that to you?'

'He knows I haven't anywhere to go'.

'But you do have a choice'.

'It's easy for you to say that. You, who've never known what I've known'.

But I've known other things. Things only I have known'.

'So, what choice have I?'

'Come with me and I'll show you'.

They walked from the city centre, across the bridge, down by the canal where plastic bags clung like prayers to the side walls, then along by the cottages that led to Lorrie's house. Children played with an old tyre on the street, rolling it along, until it wobbled and collapsed in front of them and they ran to it laughing. Lorrie brought the woman up the steps that froze in the winter, through the door with the peeling black paint. Leading her up the stairs to her bedroom, she took the photograph of her sister from the dressing table and named the face laughing out at them. She opened the wardrobe with Cecile's clothes. Spreading them out on the bed she told her to choose. She showed her the bureau where she could store her personal things, then the bed where she would sleep from now on. She showed her the cloakroom under the stairs, the log that still held up the leaning wall. Lorrie brought her to the hairdresser and they styled the woman's hair in blonde waves.

Evening is beginning to close in. The two women have reached the clubhouse.

'How can I ever thank you?' Lorrie says, kissing Cecile's fingers as they turn back towards the hotel. 'You have made my life whole again'.

'And you mine', the other woman replies. She is taller than Cecile had been, is bigger boned. She doesn't have the same soft lap as Cecile. But her hands are cool on Lorrie's forehead and when she strokes her hair she can remember.

Osmosis

You may not believe it, but I didn't always look like this. I've looked better, a lot better; have looked worse too, but my eyes are coming back from the black hollows that they were and my cheeks are not so cadaverous. This room too is returning to a semblance of what it used to be like. It was a lovely room once. Maybe it will be again.

We had dreams you see, Don and me. Yea, we had dreams. We were the ones going up in the world. Our future didn't exist in a shoebox of a flat where we had to share a stink-hole of a bathroom, with the other tenants all stuffed into that old crumbling house as well as the clients taking the stairs to the rolfer's clinic at the top of it. Hell bent on saving we went house-hunting every Sunday and came back and totted up the figures, hugging each other every time we got a hen's peck closer to our target.

Even before the earthmovers had finished digging, before cement lorries drove in, we were there checking out the view, the position of the sun, the lie of the land. We had finally found our own place. Don's car wasn't big enough to take the mountain of our belongings, so he hired Des Madden's van. A single bed was all we had, given to us by Don's aunt and that first night he held me crushed against the wall in our new peach and green bedroom. We lay, his hand holding my breast while we sipped from a single glass, the champagne that Jane gave us as a moving-in gift. We sipped until the sun went searching for the far side of the world.

And then it started.

It was raised voices at first. Don's fingers stopped their wanderings. High pitched voices carried onto a scream, there was a crash against the wall, a thump, whether body or chair we couldn't tell, any hope of Don's fingers bringing my shaking body to life destroyed. Crying broke the night and left us still searching for sleep when the clock went off.

Next morning I became a voyeur, squinting out at a neighbour in a pin-striped suit heading off to work in his new Volvo with a perfectly presented wife at his side. And so it went. Sometimes it was quiet for weeks, letting me believe that there was a home in this house. We made plans for the garden, bought hebes, cotoneaster, painted the walls of the living room, sat together on our new suite of furniture. And then there was the next eruption that pushed in against us like a wave against a quivering wall.

It went on.

In daylight they were our neighbours, he filling the bird-feeder with seeds, talking over the fence to Don on the best way to train a clematis, telling him the secret was to keep the roots cool. The secret. She would come out onto their patio and dead-head the summer plants in her beautifully cut suits. Her secretarial job often made me feel dull and uninteresting, made me believe that now as a stay-at-home mother I had lost out somewhere along the line. 'Lovely day', I would say with forked tongue, not having the gumption to ask, 'how are you after last night, how did you fare after your clothes were flung out on the lawn to be dragged all over the estate by wandering dogs'. Instead I stood there like the coward I was and fed the lie with admiration for her perfect patio plants, her Ralph Lauren shirt. What in God's honest name were we trying to gloss over, accepting his gift of Remy Martin at Christmas, wishing a happy and holy season from our house to yours.

The price of our tight lips.

Yea, it's the way it is, isn't it. Neighbours know what's going on and pull a muffler over the sounds and the sobs. Mustn't interfere, even the police would say. A private affair, a domestic matter.

'Go, Don, knock at the door, tell them we cannot put up with it'.

'No, Miriam, steer clear'.

We never could figure out what would set it off. A sunny Sunday morning, a rainy winter's afternoon, there was just never any pattern; one that we could see anyway. His voice high and coarse, spewing out 'you fuckin' bitch' through living room walls that became our children's mantra. She would turn up the television then, in a futile attempt to screen the goings-on, but do you know all it did was add to the madness.

For years we tried to push away the vile that seeped in through those paper thin walls that divided house from house. 'There but for the grace of God …' was our resolution when we didn't see eye to eye ourselves and we tiptoed round our own squall for fear it erupted into a full scale storm. Afraid that if we uncovered that side of ourselves we would in some way go tumbling down into the quagmire of next door.

'Duchess, you haven't seen her, Miriam, have you?'

'Sorry?'

'Duchess, my cat, she's missing'. Standing there at my door my neighbour was very agitated.

'No', I said, 'but if you want to check the back garden'.

She went, through the kitchen out into the back, calling Duchess, pshh, wshh. But no tiger eye shone from beneath a lavender, no marmalade body came and slunk itself against her legs.

'She's gone, if he did anything to her, I'll …'

I led her into the kitchen, filled the kettle.

She pulled out a packet of cigarettes and only when she could feel the effects of the drug did her shoulders relax.

'Don't know what I'd do without these things. If I didn't have them I'd be demented by now'. She covered her face. 'You've no idea what's going on. Christ what am I saying, you above anyone'.

I told Don that evening.

'You what?'

'I told her she should get out'.

'Over an old cat?'

'Don't be so dense, Don, do I have to spell it out for you?'

'Well, that's got nothing to do with us, Mir'.

'There you're wrong, it's affecting us even if we don't realise it, not to say what it's doing to the children'.

'But we don't know, maybe she deserv ...'

'I'll pretend I didn't hear that'.

'Well you know what they say, it takes two to tango'.

So I stopped telling him, when she called again and again, taking the pieces of paper from me with telephone numbers, pieces of information that I heard on the radio while I did the ironing in the afternoon and she was at work.

'She's been here again, that woman', Don would say when he came home in the evenings and the lingering of cigarette smoke left him sullen all evening.

'Giving her more of your expert advice', he would say. 'Let's see where that will get you'.

Where was this getting us I wondered, now that we declared allegiances?

When it began again, it went on for three nights without reprieve, starting at four in the morning. His voice was so loud, I woke up thinking there were people in our bedroom, she pleading, he cursing her out of it. All the next day it went on, the Austrian blinds never opened, keeping out the light and the eyes of passers-by who went to the shops in this quiet *cul-de-sac*.

And then she was gone.

Maybe it was the fact that she could take it herself but couldn't see it done to another living thing, especially her cat, that made her reverse the Volvo out of the driveway with her bags in the boot while his snores were lost in the closing of the hall door.

I sat on the couch for hours waiting for him to get up. Sitting, listening for the sound of a bed to creak, the first foot on the floor, a plug in a socket. I heard his footsteps on the stairs as if they were my own and then fade away as he went to the kitchen at the far end. Don used to say that newspapers tacked to wooden laths would have given us more privacy than these walls. Seeping through them, seeping as if by osmosis was the silence of this man who was left. No one to stamp on, no one to belittle. My duster swished along the mantle-piece, louder now than the sound of nothing from beyond the other side.

And here I was.

Had she told him how I had helped her, about the information I had given her, the telephone numbers? If she had, then I was trapped. Here in my own house I was a fly caught in a web. My bright sunny windows exposed me; showed me up. So I drew the heavy drapes. Would he come to my door looking for her, force it out of me? What could he be doing in there with his hands now idle, his tongue tied? I peeled onions, let them sting, diced carrots, chopped celery. I turned on the radio in the vague hope that the familiar voice of the presenter would help me. The children wondered why I had the heavy curtains drawn in the afternoon. I lied about the harshness of the light; not able to tell them that I was scared of his eyes picking me out.

I heard him switch on his television, turned down low. My telephone rang. Don was working late.

'She's gone', I whispered into the phone.

'Good riddance, maybe now we'll get some shut eye'.

All the next few days the silence like lava, flowed towards us, seering, solidifying. He left the house in darkness, came back in darkness, thinking we wouldn't notice. Then he switched the porch-light on, sure that a Volvo would crawl back into its spot. We would have given anything for the familiar, the crashing plates, the split screams, anything to protect us from this man silenced by departure.

We tried to talk, Don and me. I tried to explain to him this claw of fear that was now always at my shoulder, so that I found myself turning, checking that there was no one to strike. He didn't understand.

'You're the one that told her to go, remember; the one who gave her those numbers. Women's shelter, crowd of men bashers'.

His words were poison on arrow tips, meeting their target. Bulls-eye.

'You can't mean that, you can see what it's doing to me and to you'.

He turned from me then. 'We'd be fine if only you would pull yourself together. Go to the doctor, ask him for something for your nerves'.

I wasn't sleeping at all now, you see, wondering how we had got lost, this man and woman who had such dreams. I spent nights standing at my window in my peach and green room looking out at the street, wishing for a cardinal red Volvo to turn into the drive. Let the porch light be switched off, the television light to die.

'Come back to bed Miriam'.

'In a minute, I'll ...'

'For Christ's sake, come back right now or else ...'

And he brought his fist down on the bedside locker, dislodging bottles and creams that clattered and rolled along the floor.

Dry Bones Time

They didn't have to invite her. Even at the best of times Stella wasn't one for weddings. Cheap sherry, foolish promises, icing that sat on the teeth like cement. How many arguments did they have, one shouting 'we have to invite her' the other retaliating 'not that shriveled old bag' before the winner slid the invitation 'requesting the pleasure of' into the envelope and marked it *airmail*. Then posted it to the last of the maiden aunts who would be trussed up like a turkey at her nephew Thomas's wedding. All hoping that she wouldn't come; that she would write and they would receive a heart-felt grateful reply, about how much she would love to see everyone, but how could she travel when she couldn't get someone reliable enough to mind her precious Papillon. He would just pine away in a kennel without her. They would have been much happier with that regret, waving the healthy dollar draft for the happy couple into the air and laughing with relief. So why did she come then. Curiosity, she thought. Just to see how he had turned out.

She drank tea in houses of cousins that she had forgotten about until this, tea as thick as black sludge that coated her tongue while she choked on the word cookie. Excitement was bubbling wherever she went. Yanks and a family wedding gave birth to twinned hysteria. This was a far cry from her high-rise apartment where air came in second-hand and her garbage was gobbled up by a chute at the end of the hall. Legs that seldom stretched further than a walk along the Mall, now walked from house to other house and Boston grass that was burned yellow before summer reached July, now swathed green along the roads.

They had settled between them how she would be shared out. She could hear them say when they got her acceptance note 'if there's one thing worse than pigs in winter, it's Yanks in summer'. Then more cups of tea poured as they wondered how they would put up with her. Complaining that they would have to go out and buy orange juice and cube sugar and coloured toilet rolls; divided the burden that she was, and then no one would suffer more than the other, the Yank in summer.

It was her week to be in Margie's. She moved out of her sister Kathleen's house before the wedding so that she wouldn't be in the way. The mother of the groom needed all the space she could get; anyway it was easier for everyone, especially Thomas. Margie had rounded out since she had last seen her, with her four grown up children still hanging around her neck like a scapular. They came from their flats in town at the weekend with their dirty washing and went back with it washed and ironed. Stella wasn't going to be another burden on that string, so she refused the electric blanket and tried to cancel the daily fry. Margie, fearful that she might let it slip to one of the others over a glass of whiskey that she didn't get one, was deaf to her protests and placed the runny egg with the black pudding in front of her nonetheless. She was too thin they all squawked. There was more colour in one of her nails than in her cheeks. She needed real food, not just a paltry cup of coffee. The air reeked of burned fat while the sickly smell of alpine fresh air fresheners only helped to announce the smell of damp.

Margie said that it was ridiculous the way Kathleen was up to high doh about the wedding. Having only sons she would never know the fever of being the mother of the bride and was making up for it by fanning her flames of excitement throughout the village. Thomas, her first born, was to be married. Thomas. Stella got to see him the evening she arrived when all the relations had gathered to welcome her home. He had indeed grown into a fine man, but she couldn't mistake the thorn of dark that pierced his eye as he nodded and introduced her to his fiancée. Later when she tried to get him to talk to her he brushed her aside, put his arm around his wife-to-be and headed out into the shadow of the night. Stella was glad she didn't have to spend one hour longer in Kathleen's house. She was getting old. Drying up. Skin on her arms flopped like an old fish and reminded her of the cold withered touch that she used to feel from her own mother's arms when she was at that age.

The rain fell mercilessly on the big day even though the statue of the Child of Prague had been hidden out under the hedge. Stella was one of the first to arrive at the church. Margie didn't want to miss anything and the car wouldn't take everyone in one go. When Stella offered to get a taxi she laughed, 'You're not in Boston now, my dear'. No. She was no bother and wasn't it as easy to do two runs as one, especially as it would get Jack her husband out from under her feet. Then they wouldn't all be squashed into the Astra when they had paid such fortunes for their rig-outs.

The organist picked softly at the notes of 'Jesu Joy of Man's Desiring'. Why man's desiring she wondered, why not one about woman's desiring? That'd make them sit up and take notice. Despite herself little tears gathered at the edge of her eyelashes making the candlelight shine like stars. It was time to accept that she was one of the old relations. One of the many hauled out for the day to show the others' side that 'anything you can do, I can do better'. How much easier it would have been if she had a man on her arm. Someone who had made good, sported a gold tooth, a wide girth, a big wallet. Someone who would proclaim in a loud voice that he got into his car in the morning and drove all day and by sundown hadn't reached the outskirts of his ranch. And some well-balanced wise crack with a chip on both shoulders would say under his breath, 'I had a car like that once and had to get rid of it'.

The music swelled to fill the church. A shimmer of tulle glided up the aisle. The tall ill-at-ease frame of Thomas stepped out to take her arm. The young woman turned her head and smiled at him with faith.

The priest was big and loveless. He had forgotten their names, the best man whispering to him while feet shuffled under seats. He spoke the words of their life sentence. They looked so gullible. Now she knew why all those years ago the old relations cried. Not out of some big blow emotion of love and fidelity but that here was another pair of suckers believing that they could hold onto that feeling when skin failed and lights dimmed in their eyes. Stella played the proper part of maiden aunt. Eyes watering. The odd sniffle. The whisper of hair on the chin that even electrolysis couldn't destroy.

She kept her eye on the back of their heads. On Thomas's. His hair neatly cut for the day, dark, still curly, tipped off the edge of his jacket.

He was her first.

The couple exchanged rings. Promised honour and love. Heads behind her were whispering. Bitching day had arrived. Everyone was fair game. Kathleen's hat with the ostrich feathers; wasn't she a right show. Like something out of a circus. And the spaghetti straps of the bridesmaids' dresses. A pure disgrace. It's a wonder the priest didn't say something about them. And then she could just feel their words biting into the back of her head.

How was it that Stella never married?

Oh there was someone once, but it turned out that he had a wife up in Sligo and when he wouldn't choose between them, she upped and went off to Boston.

Christ, what an easy yarn to spin.

It was a blistering summer. Thomas was eleven. Clear bright eyes, skin so soft it hurt as she rubbed the towel along his young limbs after she took him swimming in the river. He threw off her towel and ran home ahead of her and she could think of nothing else but the sweet tanned skin of his arms where she had rubbed it dry. The soft smell of him. Kathleen thought it was great that she took such an interest in him. Even better if she brought one or two of the others as well. Stella was careful. She brought them. But she made sure that he always sat next to her so she could help him take off his coat. Feel the slim blade of his shoulder against her palm. Fix his collar. Tickle him.

One day when she arrived in her new car to take him for a drive, he refused. He was going on thirteen then. Kathleen's neck reddened with anger, telling him that he was an ungrateful pup. Stella watched her sister's knuckles turn white, draw out her hand to give him a wallop which he dodged and went running across the fields.

The married man from Sligo materialised soon after that. It was the easiest way out. They gave her a great send off. 'Poor Stella', they whispered, 'her heart must be broken' while she turned and waved to them as she went through Duty Free.

In Boston they like to come to her apartment. They see her as their mother. She gets them to do small jobs around the place; a bit of painting, sanding down, moving furniture. They come for summer while school is out. Perspiration runs like rivulets down their shoulder blades, soaking through to their t-shirts. She drinks beer with them on the balcony. Their homes are not much, they tell her. Fathers never at home, mothers bringing back strange men to their apartments. She cooks them a meal, another beer. She sits on the couch, their heads in her lap. She strokes their foreheads, along their noses, their lips. She moves her hands along their young bodies, loosens the strings of their shorts, listens to the intake of their breath as they groan with want. They tell her she's all they've ever wanted. She makes men of them.

Sometimes the super comes knocking at the door. He says the air conditioning needs checking. He is big and broad; a Polish Catholic, with a wife and seven kids in Brighton. She tells him the air conditioning is fine. As she sees him out, he catches her face and starts to kiss her. His hands are thoughtless, saying she needs a real man with plenty of experience, not a skinny kid that's still wet behind the ears. 'That's what she likes about them', she says, as she pushes him towards the door.

The ceremony was nearly over. The priest was giving his blessing. It was time they signed the register. The best man and maid of honour were called up to verify the union at a little table at the side of the altar. Signatures on a page. Thomas was gone from her now, signed over to another woman. There was a great flurry of business as the dress was settled for the photographers; the bouquet held this way and that, the bridesmaids told to turn like geese flying in formation. Posing for the album that would be on display in the pink and grey sitting room on a music stand, until the colours faded, the day lost its sheen and she became sharp and dry, he became fat and silent.

She watched him. Fine wide shoulders, the frown having given away to a shy smile, still ill-at-ease in the morning suit of a married man. How well he would have looked in t-shirt and jeans, stretched out on a chair on her balcony, sipping beer.

Stella slipped across to the pub opposite the church while the group photograph was being arranged on the steps. She wasn't the only one who had the idea. Throats were parched from the long commotion. The amber liquid eased and warmed her mouth, her throat. From the small window of the pub she could see the photographer running up and down waving his hands, trying to get a hundred and fifty guests into the lens of his camera. Stella was doing him a favour staying out of it. In years to come they would search for her in the sea of grinning faces until someone swore that her jaw-line could be seen peeking out from behind Tom Divilly and Great Aunt Julia.

The reception area was all round tables and fanned napkins. Nameplates written in gold lettering announced where everyone was to sit. They had placed her next to Margie and her husband. Distant cousins filled in the rest of the circle. There was a great clatter of chairs as the young people sat down at the table away from them. Margie's son Donal was trying to put ice cubes down the dress of a pretty young girl with long red hair. He was nearly seventeen, born after she left.

They rose and sat like car jacks all evening as they toasted every Tom Dick and Harry that ever had any dealings with either family.

Margie's cheeks were pink from sherry. It loosened her tongue in a way that it hadn't been all the time Stella stayed with her. She nodded to her husband to get another whiskey for her sister. What was she going to do with Donal? He had her heart broken. He was getting into fights; he didn't want to finish school. She wanted to get him away from the gang he was hanging around with. They were a really bad influence. And that girl he was now jig-acting with. Didn't everyone know where that would end if there wasn't a stop put to it, once and for all. She leaned over and whispered into her elder sister's ear,

'Maybe you could see your way to bringing him back with you. Just for the summer. Find him some sort of a job. Let him see a bit of the world. You know, you were always good with the young lads, Stella'.

World of Trees

To Esme it seems that the woman has caught her in her gaze. She stares out of the television so directly at her that Esme cannot look away. With her dark eyes and the way her hair falls in grey on her forehead she reminds her of Mrs. McManus who used to live in the house that backed onto theirs when she was a little girl. Esme remembers her eyes because they were the colour of earth. The same coloured eyes are looking at her again. This earth-eyed woman is saying something in a language that Esme does not understand. There is a doctor checking her heart, her pulse and over her voice the interpreter is telling the viewing world that it is the first time in four years that she has been among people. There is nothing in her face to show this. In fact she looks so ordinary you would think she was about to take out a bowl and make bread or reach down for her Brasso before she goes to polish her front door. Esme is stopped in her tracks and sits on the edge of the couch, her little daughter's sock still in her hand.

Esme leaves the room and goes out by the patio doors to the garden. There is a thumbnail of moon as clean as a nun's. The weeping willow trails down into the corner. Esme sits on the garden chair, the one with the arm tied together with an old nylon stocking and looks back at the house. There are three lights on: Beatrice's room, their own bedroom, the living room. From here she can still see the television flickering.

When Beatrice came, Paul went back on the cigarettes. He had been doing really well and had been off them for two years. Nearly. She can see his shadow, walking back and forth behind the blind in their room. He is biding his time, wondering what to do. Beatrice is lying on her bed, knees arrowed towards the ceiling, blowing clouds of smoke onto her mirror while she contemplates her next move. Beatrice always has a next move.

Beatrice had come back from London with no job and no partner. Ordinarily Esme would have been more cautious having her sister arrive at her door like that but she presented herself just as there was a crisis in the childminding arrangements. The most recent minder had rung the day before to say she was going walkabout in Australia and Esme was in a sweat as to who would look after Richard and Melanie. Beatrice was born with her life insurance policy clenched in her tiny fist and she moved into Richard's yellow room with the dinosaur curtains while Richard shared with his sister. Crisis over the house settled with relief.

Beatrice would not eat beef. No one was eating it in London now and she didn't care even if their butcher personally autographed every rump steak. She wasn't going to let her brains go spongy for anyone. If her legs were going from under her she wanted it to be a pleasurable experience and not through the consumption of burning flesh. Esme had to rearrange her weekly shopping list, fobbing off her children with turkey burgers instead. Beatrice wondered if a television would be too much trouble so Paul moved the portable from their room into the little yellow one and set it up on the pine shelf beside the wardrobe.

Esme does not like the lights shining down on her. She takes the chair with its arm in a sling and carries it in under the willow tree. The moon shines through the branches. She likes the feel of the trees, tentacles hanging down around her. No one will ever find her here. It is summer and the weather is good. She can still see out but anyone coming into the garden would think they had it to themselves. Has she the where-with-all, she wonders to sleep a sound sleep here under the tree? A makeshift home camouflaged by branches and moss. The woman from the television crosses the moon, comes in beside her.

Beatrice loved her cigarettes. She placed her Gauloises on the coffee table with the silver lighter settled neatly on top while Esme stacked the dishwasher. Paul sat watching her while she slipped the long cigarette out of its pack, placed it between her lips, let the flame engulf the tip while she drew in the air of ignition. He sat there pretending with each drag that he wasn't been drawn in. He declined her first few offers. Put his hands up in cruciform defence as if he were warding off a vampire. He was showing great discipline. Letting on it didn't matter. And then one evening Esme came in and saw twin spirals of smoke rise towards the ceiling and mingle.

The woman's shadow settles in around Esme as she hears Paul come out onto the patio and call her name. Once. Twice. She doesn't answer. Let him think she has gone. She doesn't want to talk to him. She doesn't want to hear his reasoning. Telling her it is all in her imagination. She is more interested in the television woman. What had happened to her memory? A blow, a fall, something in her family story that she didn't want to remember, a synapse that broke its connection? How did she deal with knowing of the fierce weather that was to come or the wild dogs that scavenged at night? How could she just be?

Paul carried himself differently now. He was more vocal, more lively. This wasn't the way he would normally be after three days on the road. Before Beatrice he would come in and dump his frayed temper and baggage on the floor, flop into the chair while Esme waited until he slowly became acclimatised to domesticity quicken around him. Now he came in, hung his coat in the cloakroom and poured them all a drink. Then Beatrice offered a cigarette, slipped one from the packet and his hand came across to shelter hers as she flashed open her lighter and they both drew a long satisfied sigh.

Inside the cover of the willow tree, Esme sees the woman, her teeth green from the leaves she has been chewing, the purple tint of berries on her hands. In the cold of winter did she try to burrow into the ground, roll up her body like a squirrel and wait till the earth turned and threw up the new light of Spring? How did she keep a handle on her time, pressing words out of her mind, unused, left without air unless she unleashed them onto the birds or beetles that scurried into corners? The niceties of language superfluous now like please and thank you, while her head filled green words around her. She could have sang songs to keep the wolves of panic at bay; dragging out old lullabies that never got past the first refrain before they got shadowed by her forgetting that first morning, when she just walked the length of the yard through the gap in the fence, and kept walking till she found a place deep within the trees. A world of trees that had never been felled by foresters since man first came, swallowing the dead for centuries. Wagons from 1812, bits of old leather straps and buttons scattered all around, disintegrating into moss. There she spent the day putting stones together building a shelter. A home that was to last her four years until a hunter passing through the woods came upon her, and brought her back to a world of strangers.

When Paul was away his car rested in the carport. He didn't like Esme to drive it. He was adamant that it was too big for her. Yet she watched him adjusting the seat for Beatrice so that she could reach the pedals, and when she tackled him on it he laughed and told her she was just jealous. There was no point in having a car idle in the drive when Beatrice could do the shopping and pick up the kids from their fun group on rainy days. It was just to make Esme's own life easier. Why wasn't she grateful. She wouldn't have to go out to the shops when she was just in from work. He said her imagination would be the end of her.

Esme feels the evening chill settle around her. The earth-eyed woman is lying on the ground. The cold will swell up from the earth and surge her bones. Esme takes off her cardigan and lays it on her. She covers her ears so that she won't hear the wolves baying.

She has watched him evening after evening, his eyes bright, sit across the dinner table and talk to her sister in a way that they once did together. Especially in those years before the children came along, when her cheeks were warm with wine and they didn't notice night falling slow. The look on his face then, the look on his face now. Standing at her window she studied Beatrice and himself as they came back along the path from an evening walk. He, caught between light and dark, bending his frame to catch her words thrown back up to meet him. It was the way they came in laughing, the coolness of the evening that they brought in with them, Paul rubbing his hands together to get the circulation going.

'Any chance of a cup of coffee Es? It's getting chilly out there'.

'The children are waiting for you to read them a story. You promised'.

'Couldn't you do it tonight?'

'No I couldn't'.

'Right then, be back in a min. Have the coffee ready, maybe a drop of brandy in it'.

Beatrice went over and put the kettle on. Esme stopped her as she took down the cups.

'The agency rang me today, it looks like they have a baby minder that would be suitable, so you should start looking for a real job'.

'But I thought you liked having me here. Richard and Melanie love their auntie'.

'I'm sure you would be much happier if you had your own place. Maybe London is missing you?'

'What are you trying to say to me Es'.

'Don't call me Es'.

'Right sister dear, out with it'.

'Are you sleeping with Paul?'

'What on earth makes you ask that?'

'Well are you?'

'I think your husband is the best one to answer that'.

Esme climbs the stairs. She hears Paul reading for their children. She stands at their door. Paul is finishing the story. The Billy Goats Gruff are getting the better of the troll and when they kick him up in the air, he burns up as he falls back through the atmosphere. Richard has his thumb in his mouth, Melanie is already asleep. She bends and picks up Melanie's sock that is on the floor by the door-frame. She sees the marks on the door that measure their spurts of growth. There is Richard's and below him Melanie's. Two new marks have been etched into the stripped pine, way above their children's. Paul's at five foot eleven and below that by a good three inches, Beatrice's. They have carved themselves forever into her house.

She is standing in the bathroom screaming at Paul. He tells her she is imagining things. Beatrice is his sister-in-law, for Christ's sake. She challenges him about the carving on the children's door frame. He laughs. Only a bit of fun. But his name is lying on top of hers. The way he wants it to be. She asks him has he slept with her. He says no. She wants to believe him, but she knows by the way he holds his head and rubs his index finger along his top lip that it's not the full truth. It is what he has committed in his heart that is.

She tells him that she has found a new childminder. That they don't need Beatrice's services any more. She sees the look of hate sear across his face, then it is gone. He has always left the childminding arrangements to her. He cannot argue this one. She leaves and goes downstairs. The light is on in Beatrice's room. As she goes through the living room she is stopped by the earth-eyed woman.

From her covert, she watches this woman come back after four years with the spirit to pick up the pieces. Search the faces of village people that might have the same line of jaw, the same forehead, the same colour eyes, so that she could tell they were from her own lineage. Esme draws this spirit towards her, clasps it to herself as she sees the light go out in their bedroom. Paul walking along the corridor. Knocking on Beatrice's door. Going into the room with its yellow walls and dinosaurs and lying the full length of the bed with her.